Y0-BCW-938

Plus

Healthy Teeth

Loose Tooth

by Mari Schuh

Consulting Editor:
Gail Saunders-Smith, PhD

Consultant:
Lori Gagliardi CDA, RDA, RDH, EdD

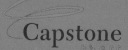
Capstone
press

Mankato, Minnesota

Pebble Plus is published by Capstone Press,
151 Good Counsel Drive, P.O. Box 669, Mankato, Minnesota 56002.
www.capstonepress.com

1 2 3 4 5 6 13 12 11 10 09 08

Library of Congress Cataloging-in-Publication Data
Schuh, Mari C., 1975–
    Loose tooth/by Mari Schuh.
    p. cm. — (Pebble plus. Healthy teeth)
    Summary: "Simple text, photographs, and diagrams present information about having a loose tooth,
including how they feel and how to take care of all teeth properly"— Provided by publisher.
    Includes bibliographical references and index.
    ISBN-13: 978-1-4296-1243-2 (hardcover)
    ISBN-10: 1-4296-1243-6 (hardcover)
    ISBN-13: 978-1-4296-1789-5 (softcover)
    ISBN-10: 1-4296-1789-6 (softcover)
    1. Teeth — Mobility — Juvenile literature. 2. Teeth — Care and hygiene — Juvenile literature.
I. Title. II. Series.
RK63.M368 2008
617.6'01 — dc22   2007027208

Editorial Credits
Sarah L. Schuette, editor; Veronica Bianchini, designer

Photo Credits
Capstone Press/Karon Dubke, all

The author dedicates this book to her parents, Mona and Daniel Schuh, of Fairmont, Minnesota.

Note to Parents and Teachers

The Healthy Teeth set supports national science standards related to personal health. This book describes and illustrates what it's like to have a loose tooth. The images support early readers in understanding the text. The repetition of words and phrases helps early readers learn new words. This book also introduces early readers to subject-specific vocabulary words, which are defined in the Glossary section. Early readers may need assistance to read some words and to use the Table of Contents, Glossary, Read More, Internet Sites, and Index sections of the book.

Table of Contents

Teeth

Having a loose tooth is part of growing up. Andy was 5 when his first baby tooth became loose.

A permanent tooth
inside Andy's gums
pushed on his baby tooth.
The loose tooth fell out.

A permanent tooth grew
into the empty space.
Andy will have 32 permanent
teeth when he is an adult.

How It Feels

Having loose teeth
can feel funny.
Andy has two loose teeth
that he wiggles
with his tongue.

Loose teeth make it hard
to eat some foods.
Andy has trouble biting
into a hard apple.

Andy eats soft foods like yogurt instead.

Nutrition Facts

Serving Size
1 container (142g)

Servings 1

Calories 100

Fat Cal. 0

*Percent Daily Values (DV) are
based on a 2,000 calorie diet.

Amount/Serving	%DV*	Amount/Serving	%DV*
Total Fat 0g	0%	Total Carb 22g	
Sat. Fat 0g	0%	Fiber 0g	
Trans Fat 0g		Sugars 8g	
Cholest. 0mg	0%	Protein 5g	
Sodium 70mg	3%		

Vitamin A 0% • Vitamin C 0% • Calcium 8% •

INGREDIENTS: CULTURED NONFAT MILK, SUGAR, STRAWBERRIES
FRUCTOSE CORN SYRUP, STRAWBERRIES, WATER, STRAWBERRY FRUIT BASE INCL
CITRIC ACID, NATURAL FLAVOR, RED 40), FOOD STARCH-MODIFIED
POTASSIUM SORBATE (A PRESERVATIVE).

THIS ENTIRE PACKAGE IS COPYRIGHTED ©2004 KEMPS, LLC
GENERAL OFFICES, MINNEAPOLIS, MN 55414
www.kemps.com CONSUMER HOTLINE 1(800) 726-6455
ACTIVE YOGURT CULTURES GRADE A • PASTEURIZED PLANT 27-167

Loose teeth sometimes
hurt a little.
Andy's mouth feels better
in a few days.

Healthy Teeth

Having healthy teeth means having a healthy smile. Andy makes sure he brushes and flosses every day.

You can take care
of your teeth too.
Soon, you'll have
a whole new smile!

Glossary

baby teeth — the first teeth you have; baby teeth are also called primary teeth.

floss — to pull a thin piece of dental floss between your teeth to help keep your teeth clean

gum — the firm skin around the base of teeth

permanent teeth — the teeth you have your whole life, after your baby teeth; permanent teeth are also called adult teeth.

tongue — a muscle in your mouth you can move

wiggle — to move something up and down or side to side just a little bit

Read More

Curry, Don L. *Take Care of Your Teeth.* Rookie Read-About Health. New York: Children's Press, 2005.

DeGezelle, Terri. *Taking Care of My Teeth.* Keeping Healthy. Mankato, Minn.: Capstone Press, 2006.

Goulding, Sylvia. *Taking Care of Your Teeth.* Healthy Kids. Vero Beach, Fla.: Rourke, 2005.

Internet Sites

FactHound offers a safe, fun way to find Internet sites related to this book. All of the sites on FactHound have been researched by our staff.

Here's how:

1. Visit *www.facthound.com*

2. Choose your grade level.

3. Type in this book ID **1429612436** for age-appropriate sites. You may also browse subjects by clicking on letters, or by clicking on pictures and words.

4. Click on the **Fetch It** button.

FactHound will fetch the best sites for you!

Index

Word Count: 141
Grade: 1
Early-Intervention Level: 18